# Valentine & Orson

# Valentine & Orson

Re-created as a folk play in verse and paintings by

## NANCY EKHOLM BURKERT

A Floyd Yearout Book

FARRAR, STRAUS AND GIROUX • NEW YORK

# For Rand

# Valentine & Orson

*We bring before you now a play, by means*
*Of pantomime, in nine momentous scenes.*
*The present year is 1555, a day*
*In Flanders, after planting time, in May.*
*Our story, though, is found in ancient lore,*
*Two hundred years ago, or long before.*

## THE PLAYERS

Narrator, Pacolet . . . . . . . . . . . . . . . . . . . . . . PACOLET

Alexander (Emperor of Greece), Ferragus (The Giant) . . . . . FATHER

Bellisant (the Elder), The Lion . . . . . . . . . . . . . . . MOTHER

Bellisant (the Younger), Clerymond, Fezon . . . . . . . . . DAUGHTER

The False Archbishop, The Bear, Valentine, and Orson . . . TWIN SONS

Blandyman, The Green Knight, The Churl . . . . . . . . . . A FARMER

ALSO APPEARING: *Men, women, and children of the village*
*as King Pepin, the cook, the merchant, the oracle, angels, musicians, and peasants.*
*A cart horse and farm animals.*

# PROLOGUE

AH, FRIENDS, *both great and small, come near!*
*The right good troupe of players you see here*
*Will mime a tale that you shall not forget,*
*With verse recited by your Pacolet,*
*Of* ORSON *and his brother,* VALENTINE.
*Now place a coin in that clay bag of mine*
*And gather round. Our tale begins in days*
*When Pepin ruled as King of France, and praise*
*Was heard of his young sister, Bellisant.*
*This lady was, in all, so excellent*
*That rhymers, like myself, and troubadours*

*Sang lays at court, and on such distant shores*
*That Alexander, Emperor of Greece,*
*Fell ardently in love and had no peace!*
*He came to France in pomp and rich array*
*And asked to marry her. Good folk, they say*
*The King gave his consent most willingly*
*For he was honored by this chance to be*
*With such exalted power well allied.*
*Thus, Bellisant became the Emperor's bride.*
*But, friends, when we begin an enterprise*
*Can anyone predict where Fortune lies?*

With wind at will,
The royal couple sailed
To Constantinople,
Where they were hailed
By joyous crowds along
The shore, who spied
Their noble sovereign
And his graceful bride.

These two were loved and reigned in harmony.
✤ But evil came to them, as you shall see,
Because the Emperor unwisely chose
To place his trust in one you would suppose
To be above all vice, the virtuous
Archbishop. Sad to say, it happened thus:
This holy man, his monarch's confidant,
Was faithless when he gazed on Bellisant
And fell into the flames of earthly love.
One day he smiled, and sat quite near, whereof
She paid no heed, until he said, "My dear,
Most high and sovereign lady, you see here
Your chaplain, and your humble servant, too.
I suffer night and day with thoughts of you.
Your eyes! Your face! Of God I now require
That He will give you courage and desire

To take me as your lover. Have no fear
That He will judge you. As His vicar here,
I give you absolution easily."
The lady, shocked to hear such treachery
From one so trusted in that house, declared,
"You are a false Archbishop to have dared
These wicked words. I see the Emperor
Has elevated you in honor more
Than you deserve. He trusts you in all things.
But you would taint the blood of France, of kings,
From whom I am descended. You extol
My virtues, but would trifle with my soul!
You must forget this foolish sentiment
Or I shall tell my husband your intent."
✤ The false Archbishop saw no comfort now.
He was refused and scorned, and thought, somehow,
To hide his evil deed and save his pride.
He slyly drew the Emperor aside,
And feigning loyalty, he whispered, "Sire,
You know your welfare is my sole desire.
As counselor and confidant, I say
Your wife now loves another. This I learned by way
Of his confession, thus his name I cannot tell.
The princes gossip in the court, as well,

That you had thought to take into your bed
A pure and gentle maiden. But instead
You have a harlot. Now, at any cost,
Correct her, or I deem your honor lost."
Bad bones and blight! The Emperor believed
The traitor's story and was so aggrieved
He wept, and ached with sorrow for his wife.
You see, he loved her as he loved his life!
But soon his anger flared. He lost all reason,
Cursing, and accusing her of treason.
"I have been told about your sin!" he railed,
Abusing her with rage until she wailed
So high the court ran quickly to her side.
The lady, wounded by her love, denied
His accusation. Many voices rose
In her defense. "I see now how it goes!"
Exclaimed the Emperor, "And I decree
A painful death to all who disagree!"
One baron, brave and wise, addressed him thus:
"Ah, Sire, your wife is much beloved by us
And she is great with child, most certainly
By your own deed. Pray treat her tenderly.
If you continue to be cruel and rough,
Her brother will avenge her, soon enough!"

The Empress wept and begged, upon her knees,
"My Lord, have pity. Listen to my pleas
And spare our child. Confine me in a tower
Until I am delivered. At that hour
You may do with me whatever that you will."
Her words had no effect. The Emperor, still
Profoundly hurt to think he was betrayed,
Remained so fierce the barons were afraid,
And led the lady from her husband's ire.
They summoned Blandyman, the loyal squire
Who had attended her from France and served
In every need. With pity, he observed
Her sorrowful estate. And with alarm!
He feared the Emperor would do more harm.
So he beseeched her, "Let us go at once
To Pepin, who will keep you safe in France."
"To flee in haste," she answered, "would imply
That I am guilty. I would rather die
Than earn such blame when I am innocent."
✠ It was not long before the Emperor sent
A guard to bring his wife. His heart was sore
With anguish, and he trembled all the more.
"For Pepin's sake, your life is spared," he said.
If truth be told, he loved her still. Instead

He spoke these fatal words: "I banish you
From all of Greece, and from my empire, too!"
Obeying this command, with no delay,
Bellisant and Blandyman went on their way,
While tears of grief and pity followed them
As in a wake. The great and least of men
Lamented when they saw pass through the gate,
Into the fields, a lady crushed by fate.
Her joy had changed so swiftly to distress,
Her songs to sighs, her life to loneliness. ❖

The false Archbishop
Watched the two depart,
Still coveting the lady
In his heart.
He changed his vestments
For a cloak and sword,
And rode out, hastened
By desire, toward
The wood. He swiftly overtook his prey,
Who recognized her foe with great dismay.
Alighting from his horse, he said to her,
"Dear Lady, now I see the Emperor
Has driven you away. If you agree
To take me as your lover, you shall see
That I can use my power to restore
Your first estate, exalted as before."
He leaned to kiss her, and when Blandyman
Repelled him with his staff, a fight began!
A passing merchant happened on the scene.
He bade them to desist and stepped between
The foes to settle who was wrong or right.
He quickly learned about the lady's plight,
And warned the traitor, who had turned to flee,
That death was the reward for treachery!

"May I be granted life, until the time
When I shall see him punished for this crime,"
Declared the merchant as he rode away.
They gave him thanks for all he did that day.
✤ Their flight resumed, when they had taken rest,
Through many foreign realms, and riding west,
The fugitives at last arrived in France.
They passed through Orléans, and six miles hence,
Were deep inside a forest, dark and overgrown,
When Bellisant, dismounting with a moan,
Implored, "Go find a midwife now, I pray.
I feel I must give birth without delay!"
The squire placed the lady on her cloak
Upon a level space beneath an oak
Which he marked well. He rode off in the wood
To seek some help, as swiftly as he could.
✤ It happened by a strange coincidence
That Pepin rode that day from Paris, thence,
To visit Bellisant in Greece. He came into
The forest with his royal retinue
And could not know his sister's presence there.
Now, whom should he encounter but her squire,
Who reined his horse at once to greet the King.
"Blandyman, fair sir, what tidings do you bring

From Constantinople?" "Sire," said Blandyman,
"I fear no word is good," and he began
To weep, as he described the tragedy.
King Pepin interrupted angrily,
Defending not his sister as he ought
But siding with the Emperor! He thought
His ties with Bellisant were at an end,
As well as his alliance with a friend.
He rudely spurred his horse, reversed his way,
Rebuffed all else he should have heard that day.
The squire did not attempt to tell him more
But rode upon his mission as before.
❀ The mysteries of fate and fortune played,
As Bellisant, alone in labor, prayed
For God to comfort her, while she gave birth.
Not one, but two fair sons were born on earth!
She cried, and laughed with joy to hold them near,
When suddenly her joy was changed to fear!
A huge brown bear loomed up and took one child
In its great jaws, then plunged into the wild!
The lady followed it on hands and knees.
Alas! The bear had vanished. When her pleas
Were echoed by a distant, tiny wail,
She tried to find her child, to no avail.

A sickness overcame the lady there.
Confused and lost, she fainted from despair.
❀ Her brother, meantime, rode in much distress
Of heart and mind, back through the wilderness,
And passed, by chance, a certain lofty tree.
He glanced aside and was amazed to see
What lay beside it! "Lords," called out the King,
"By God, who has created everything,
Come see a babe that was abandoned here."
"Sir King," exclaimed the lords, as they drew near,
"You speak the truth!" The crying newborn child
Was given to the care of Pepin's mild
And able squire, Valentine, by name,
Who later called his little charge the same.
King Pepin solemnly proclaimed, "From hence
He shall be nourished at my own expense
And nobly kept, while God shall grant him life,
As if wellborn, of me and of my wife."
This was his nephew, but he could not know.
I say he had good cause to love him so!
❀ Our players will assemble presently,
To show you what had happened by the tree;
Poor Bellisant, her children, and the bear,
The King, surprised, as he was riding there!

✠ When Blandyman returned, he brought
A midwife to assist the birth. He thought
To find his lady near the tree. Instead,
They searched, and found her, lying as if dead,
So far away that nothing could explain
What might have brought her there. With pain
She told them everything. "We must retrace
My way," she moaned, "for I must find the place
My other child abides." The squire replied,
"But I was there and looked on every side.
I saw no child. Dear Madame, lean on me
And we shall search together by the tree."
Her sons were gone. Your Pacolet is sure
That Allah mourns what human hearts endure. ✤

**3** Bellisant was guided
To a village where
The midwife bathed
And tended her with care
Until she was well mended.
For her grief
There was no remedy
And no relief,
But it is often said we cannot feel
A sorrow time, in passing, does not heal.
Adversity was doubled when she learned
From Blandyman's account that she was spurned
By her own brother, Pepin! In dismay,
She vowed to find a country far away
Where none would know of her disgrace and none
Could ever learn her fate. With Blandyman
She wandered over land and sea, until
Fair winds delivered them to Portugal.
They sailed into a port and, as they moored,
Were frightened when a giant came aboard!
He was so great and powerful, no horse
Could hold his weight. His name was Ferragus,
And it had been his custom to demand
A tribute from those coming to his land.

But when he spied the noble passenger,
He led the lady, followed by her squire,
To greet his wife, who saw the stranger's grace,
Her gentle bearing, and the kindly face
Of Blandyman, and welcomed them to stay.
It was fair haven they had found that day!
✤ A dozen years passed by. Now you shall hear
How falsehood will forever reappear
To claim its maker. The Archbishop had attained
Still greater influence and he restrained
The Emperor from feelings of regret
And longing for his wife. "Do not forget
That it was she by whom you were betrayed!"
The villain counseled and he was obeyed.
It happened that an autumn fair was planned,
And many merchants came, from every land.
The false Archbishop, sent to rule the fair
With several hundred men of arms, saw there
The noble merchant we have come to know,
Who rescued Bellisant. The traitor's foe!
He was supplied with cloth of silk and gold,
And when the fair was ended, he had sold
More goods than anyone. The traitor sent
His sergeant, who demanded, "Pay one tenth

On all you sold, to us!'' The merchant said,
"I will not!'' and they traded blows instead!
This caused a great commotion at the fair.
The merchant, at the traitor's mercy there,
Was nearly put to death without delay.
But he was well advised in law, that is to say,
He asked that he be heard in his defense.
At first, his acts of disobedience
Were put, by the Archbishop, to the court.
Then he was given license to retort.
And when he thoroughly explained his case,
Imagine how the look on every face
Was changed to horror, as the treachery,
The wicked lies, and vile disloyalty
Of that most false Archbishop were exposed.
But he denied it all, as we supposed!
The merchant pledged to take the field and fight
So justice could prevail, and prove him right.
When they had set the day, the Emperor advised
King Pepin of this urgent enterprise
And he arrived there, in good time to see
The fight begin. The foes fought bitterly
And blood was spilled before the sun's retreat.
By Allah, friends, the traitor met defeat!

Now keepers of the field were told to bring
The Emperor, all lords and barons, and the King
To hear the traitor's words, as he confessed!
Ah, then they knew the lady they loved best
Was lost by treachery, and by belief
Too lightly given. Joy was marred by grief.
The Emperor knelt down before the King,
Who raised him and forgave him everything.
Their peace was made. Their sole intent became
To find the lady and restore her name.
⌘ The King returned to France by sea and land,
To Orléans, and there, a feast was planned
In welcome. When the hour came to dine,
The squire, who had charge of Valentine,
Presented him most proudly to the King.
"Sire, this orphan child I have been nurturing
Is twelve, but in a few years' time will be
Full grown. I now beseech your majesty
To ponder this.'' King Pepin thanked him well,
For from the child's demeanor he could tell
His virtue. Valentine was, rightfully,
Made welcome in the royal family.
The boy grew tall, expert in every skill,
And favored by the King for his good will.

He was a foundling, yes, but nobly blessed.
✠ As for his brother's fate, I can attest
The other babe was carried by the bear
Into a deep and gloomy cavern, where
She dropped him for her little cubs to eat.
Ah, friends, to see a miracle is sweet!
Instead, they stroked him gently with their paws,
And played, which gave their mother cause
To take some care. And so she pulled him near
And nursed him like the others for a year.
He soon grew strong, and rugged as a bear,
While prowling far and wide outside the lair.
Exploring in the forest, he would prey
On beasts, or any man, who passed that way!
✠ At fifteen years, so great was his renown
That many tried, but failed, to hunt him down.
He wore no cloth and could not speak a word,
Although he understood all sounds he heard.
Indeed, it seemed he was less man than bear
And so they called him ORSON everywhere. ✤

Now, here was Valentine,
In high repute,
His brother, Orson,
Infamous, a brute,
Who roamed the wild
Without restraint.
As three years passed, each
Day there was complaint
By some poor countryman that Orson seized.
The King and all his barons, right displeased,
Held council for advice, and they were told
To make it known a thousand coins of gold
Were offered for the Wild Man, quick or dead!
A number of brave knights arrived, in dread
Of Orson, but inspired by the prize.
A pair of Pepin's sons were there whose eyes
Were fixed upon their father's property,
Who envied Valentine his love. In mockery
They called him "foundling," daring him to prove
He was of noble character and brave
By being first to seek the Wild Man. The King
Knew their malicious taunt could bring
Sure death to Valentine, and he reproved
Them strongly. Valentine was sadly moved,

For he had borne good will to them, and said
That he would capture Orson, quick or dead.
"My child, consider what you do!" exclaimed
The fearful King. "For he cannot be tamed.
To suffer words, from those who envy us,
Or from false tongues, would be more virtuous."
"Ah, Sire," said Valentine, "I undertake
This enterprise for my own honor's sake.
They call me 'foundling' with a show of scorn.
I know not who I am, or wherefore I was born
Inside the wood, or from what place I came.
I pray, someday, to know my parents' name."
King Pepin wept, bereft, as you could tell,
And both, in one voice, said, "God keep thee well."
✤ Now Valentine, with one old squire, rode
Upon the morrow toward the dark, wild wood
Where Orson roamed. He entered there, alone,
And searched all day, but when the sun went down,
He tied his horse to browse beneath a tree,
And took some bread and wine. Then, prudently,
As dusk gave way to darkest night, he crept
Into the branches of the tree, and slept
Till dawn. When he awoke, he looked around,
And saw a beast approaching on the ground.

Save us! What a sight! It was the Wild Man!
Suddenly he stopped, crouched low, and ran
To touch the horse he spied beneath a tree.
A horse so fair and beautiful to see
That Orson combed it in a friendly way.
At once the frightened steed began to neigh,
To kick the stranger, flinging all about.
So Orson pulled it down but heard a shout,
"Leave my horse alone!" and lifting up his eyes
He spied a man and grunted in surprise.
He bared his teeth and fiercely shook his fists
To show that he would tear the man to bits!
Then Valentine leaped down and drew his sword,
But Orson ducked the stroke, and running toward
His foe, he cast him down with simple strength
Upon the ground. They wrestled, but at length
It could be seen that Orson was too strong,
And Valentine would not survive for long.
He pulled his hunting knife and thrust it wide,
Which made a painful wound in Orson's side.
A howl of rage resounded in the wood
As Orson ran, with all the force he could,
To cast his foe upon the ground again,
Assailing him with nails and teeth. But then

He wrenched away the painted shield and gazed
A moment at its colors, much amazed.
Brave Valentine renewed his fierce attack.
He swung his sword at Orson, who leaped back
And quickly bent and broke a sturdy tree,
Which made a dreadful club. Ah, woe is me!
For now a deadly battle had begun
Which held no victory for either one.
⌘ Your Pacolet will not recount to you
The brutal ways they fought, for neither knew
He sought to slay his brother, furthermore,
That they were twins, born eighteen years before.
Becoming faint and weary, both gave way
To take some breath. Praise Allah, I can say,
That staring deep into each other's eyes,
They felt a vivid sense of kinship rise.
For in his enemy, each one could see
A being not unlike himself! Softly
Valentine said, "Orson, come with me, be wise.
Let me provide for thee. Salvation lies
In peace, and faith, which I shall teach to thee.
And thou shalt live thy life more honestly
As everybody should!" The Wild Man understood
These quiet words to mean not harm, but good.

He knelt upon the earth, for he was drawn
By his true nature, as the light of dawn
Transforms the night. The two foes made amends
By reaching out their hands to touch, as friends,
The shoulders of the other. Ah! How could
They help but feel the bond of brotherhood.
When we set out to conquer, we retreat
From harmony, which is the greater feat.
This moment, Pacolet will have you know,
Is hallowed, as our worthy players show. ❖

## 5

By subtle signs and words
The Wild Man knew
Whatever Valentine
Would have him do.
He led the way
Until they stood outside
The wood. And then
He meekly loped beside
The splendid horse, as harmless as a lamb.
⌘ Along the route to Orléans, they came
Into a village where the very sight
Of Orson's shaggy face caused such a fright,
A din of slamming gates and snarling dogs,
Of hissing geese and loudly grunting hogs
Was all they heard in greeting. "Have no fear!"
Cried Valentine. "Pray give us lodging here."
But no one answered him, for no one dared
To harbor Orson. Valentine despaired
Of finding rest. He let the Wild Man break
Into a hostelry, so they could take
Some shelter there. The folk who hid within
Ran out the back when Orson sauntered in.
Then he and Valentine looked all around
And came into the kitchen, where they found
Some meat and fowl were threaded on a spit
Before the fire. Valentine was turning it
When Orson tore the uncooked meat away,
Devouring it as beasts would eat their prey.
He finished, panting, for he felt a thirst
And, from a water cauldron, drank headfirst
As horses do beside a stream. Valentine
Led Orson to the cellar, drew some wine
Into a pot, and watched him drink the whole.
Soon Orson wanted more and poured a bowl
To carry to the horse, because he thought
That it would like some, too! But he was caught
Midway, by Valentine, who shook his head!
So Orson drank the rest himself, instead.
He lay upon the hearth, and soon he slept
So deeply that his friend, who wisely kept
A watchful eye, observed, "He may be wild,
And strong, but now he sleeps just like a child.
What if I poke him with my foot, in jest,
Pretending there are folk about?" This test
So startled Orson that he grabbed a log
And rammed the doorway, howling like a dog.
Valentine laughed loudly, whereby Orson knew
It was a trick to see what he could do.

Again he slept, the log gripped near his chest,
But Valentine kept watch and did not rest,
Because the Wild Man's howl had caused alarm.
The village folk had left their homes to arm
And bells of warning tolled throughout the night.
But no one dared attack. When it was light
The friends departed peaceably and made
Their way to Orléans, where Pepin often stayed.
❀ When townfolk spied the savage Orson, led
By Valentine, they shrieked and quickly fled.
"Long live the hardy Valentine!" they cried
From high up in their windows, well inside!
Then Valentine and Orson crossed the town
But found the palace gates had been closed down
Because the porters were afraid. "Do not fear,"
He called out. "Tell King Pepin I am here.
Upon my life, I say to all within this realm
That Orson means no earthly creature harm."
The King rejoiced to have this news, and thought,
Assuredly, a miracle was wrought!
The court assembled as the gates were raised,
And Valentine was roundly cheered and praised,
Though Pepin's heirs remained his enemies.
Wild Orson, grinning proudly, stood at ease,

While lords and ladies stared, in curiosity.
The King exclaimed, "How marvelous to see
This man, who is well made and of good height.
Arrayed, he would appear a right fair knight!"
❀ A feast was soon arranged, and had begun
When Orson entered, watched by everyone
Inside the hall. He saw one servant bring
A peacock on a platter for the King.
He snatched it off and, crouching on the floor,
Consumed it like a wolf, but wanted more,
Devouring meat and fish before he seized
Some wine and drank it freely as he pleased.
But when he raised the pot and threw it down
To smash it, everybody gasped! A frown
From Valentine made Orson feel ashamed,
But Pepin laughed, and to them all exclaimed,
"He gives me pleasure. Let the Wild Man be!"
❀ But there was further mischief. He was free
To roam the royal gardens, climb the trees,
Play games among the children, and to tease
The ladies of the court. All those in dread
Of Orson were amused by him, instead!
But one day, he was prowling here and there,
And came upon the palace kitchen, where

The cook prepared some capons for the fire.
Orson grabbed two birds, consuming both entire!
The cook took up a pestle, struck him on the head,
And here you see what happened! Rumor spread
That Pepin's cook was nearly slain. "This time
The Wild Man shall be punished for his crime!"
Declared the King. But Orson fetched the weapon
That the cook had used, and when King Pepin
Understood the case, he pardoned both of them.
✠ Valentine took charge of Orson, teaching him
The ways he should behave, and in that land
He was protected by the King's command.
They stayed in Pepin's court a year or two.
That he could be their uncle, no one knew! ✤

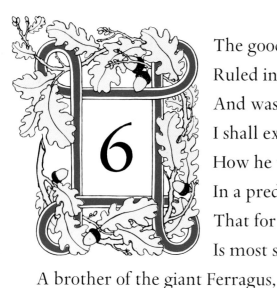

The good Duke Savary
Ruled in Aquitaine
And was King Pepin's friend.
I shall explain
How he was caught
In a predicament
That for our tale
Is most significant!
A brother of the giant Ferragus,
Renowned as the "Green Knight," and infamous,
Laid siege against the Duke and all his land.
He held him hostage, with but one demand:
"Give me your daughter, Fezon, for my wife,
Or I will burn your land and take your life!
I shall depart, if you can find a knight
To challenge and defeat me in a fight!"
Duke Savary sent letters everywhere.
But in King Pepin's court no one would dare
To undertake the cause, save Valentine,
Who in his heart had never ceased to pine
For knowledge of his own nativity.
This was a splendid opportunity
To search in realms outside of France, and find
Some tidings of his birth to ease his mind.

He felt obliged, moreover, to defend
The noble man who was King Pepin's friend.
✠ Wild Orson ran beside him, on the route
Toward Aquitaine, and all the world ran out,
Amused to see a man so like a bear,
All rough, and nearly naked. He could hear
Their laughter but the Wild Man paid no heed.
However, Valentine could see his need
And found an armorer nearby who made
A coat of mail, in finest steel. He bade
That Orson pull it on, and ever thence,
The Wild Man had a prouder countenance!
✠ They journeyed on, two fellows glad to be
Companions on the road, and soon could see
The spires of Aquitaine, which rose on high.
By chance, or fate, an aged man passed by
Who had a long white beard and the attire
Of a pilgrim. Actually, he was a squire
On his way from Portugal to France, carrying
A noble lady's message to the King.
He warned them not to enter Aquitaine,
Where forty knights were overcome and slain.
They could be seen, afar, hanging from a tree.
And then, as they were parting company,

Valentine was strangely drawn to this old man,
Who was, as you have guessed, good Blandyman.
✤ They ventured on and soon arrived before
The Duke and his fair daughter. Gathered there
Were fourteen other knights from foreign lands,
To challenge the Green Knight and his demands.
Valentine spoke reverently to Fezon:
"Right dear Lady, I have come from Pepin,
Mighty King of France, and with me, here,
The bravest man on earth. He has no peer."
The maiden gazed upon the simply clad
And rugged Orson. Ah, we hear it said
That when the heart is dealt a blow, no love
Is less than beautiful. And, friends, above
All others, Fezon set her heart on Orson!
"A thousand thanks to both of you," said Fezon.
"Too many noble knights were slain for me.
I beg you not to put your lives in jeopardy!"
But Orson placed his hands across his heart,
And Valentine insisted, for their part.
✤ Thus on the morrow, sixteen men in all
Took counsel with each other in the hall.
The two who asked that they be first to fight
Were soon defeated by the fierce Green Knight,

Who hung them without mercy from the tree.
Now Orson shook his fists ferociously,
But Valentine was next, and when he rode
Onto the field, the evildoer crowed,
"Ha, Knight! On yonder rowan tree, you see
A green shield hanging. Bring it here to me!"
Valentine retorted, "Why? Do I observe
That you have servants? Why not let them serve!"
The villain shouted, "You shall fetch the shield,
Or by my law, we shall not take the field!"
So Valentine complied in fear his foe would try
To use this lame excuse, but could not pry
The shield away. "Now you will understand,"
The villain jeered, "this shield from Fairyland
Will not come loose unless you are the one
Predestined as my conqueror, the son
Of royal rank, but nourished well without
A woman's milk!" "What you have said I doubt
Is true of me," lamented Valentine, "yet
I shall fight!" "Such folly reaps regret,"
The Green Knight said and spurred his horse.
The two fought back and forth along the course
So fiercely all their weapons broke apart.
They stopped as darkness fell, but vowed to start

When it was day. They had sore wounds to tend.
The Green Knight kept a magic balm to mend
His injuries, but this he kept concealed.
Poor Valentine was not so quickly healed.
When he had dressed his wounds, he tried to rest,
But could not sleep as he reviewed his quest
To learn the truth about his origin.
He thought of the enchanted shield, of Orson;
Was he by chance or by a jest of fate
Somehow descended from a high estate?
⌘ At dawn, it could be seen that Valentine
Was in a melancholy state of mind.
He gathered all his armor for the fight,
But, friends, imagine Orson's wild delight
When Valentine came forth to place it all
Into his hands! Orson, prancing round the hall,
Made signs that he preferred a club of wood
To other weapons, but he understood
The reason he must pose as Valentine.
The shining armor made him look so fine
That all who saw him clapped and cheered, except
His wounded friend, who was forlorn and kept
An anxious watch as Orson rode away,
And prayed for his return, unharmed, that day. ✤

The Green Knight scowled
To see his foe draw near
And touch the Green
Pavilion with his spear,
A silent signal of
Defiance that enraged
This haughty knight.
The two were soon engaged
So savagely that I, your Pacolet,
To make the shortest speech of horror yet,
Will only comment that much blood was shed.
Orson rolled his eyes, and shook his shaggy head.
While injuring his foe right grievously.
Alas, he was abashed when he could see
The Green Knight's wounds were somehow healed!
He threw away all weaponry, to wield
His own two arms alone. With simple force
He pinned the knight, who in due course
Was made to gasp, "Have mercy! I will yield!"
Now, Valentine rode out upon the field
To spare his life. Berating him, he said,
"On yonder tree, too many men hang dead,
And from the highest branch, you too shall sway,
Unless you heed our laws, renounce your ways,

And give allegiance to the King of France."
The Green Knight, seeing this his final chance,
Agreed. When he had promised with his oath,
They let him rise. He recognized that both
These men had fought with him. "Yes, it is true,"
Said Valentine, "I shall not lie to you."
"Then let this other man retrieve the shield!"
The Green Knight cried. Orson crossed the field,
His arm held forth, and as he neared the tree,
The shield leaped to his hand immediately!
The Green Knight, falling to his knees, exclaimed,
"You are the one that Destiny has named
To conquer me, and all I said of you,
Of your nativity and life, is true.
Should you need further proof, I recommend
You seek my gracious sister, Clerymond,
Who, in her castle, keeps a Head of Brass
Which tells of everything that comes to pass.
And now, as I have promised, I command
My forces to disarm, and leave this land."
In Aquitaine, the little and the great
Engaged in sports and plays, to celebrate,
Not least, their joy in the betrothal of
The Lady Fezon to her only love.

⌘ About this time, old Blandyman reached France
And spoke to Pepin with slight deference!
"Most noble King, the lady that I serve
Is your own sister. She did not deserve
The shame of exile, nor the cruelty
Of your misguided heart!" Remorsefully
King Pepin sighed and softly begged to know
Where he could find her. Blandyman was slow
To answer. "I have promised not to tell.
If you still doubt her honor in this quarrel,
A friend stands by to fight in her defense."
"There has been proof enough of innocence,"
Replied the King, "and honor is retrieved.
The traitor has confessed. But I was grieved
To learn that when my sister was exiled
Her husband knew that she was great with child.
We do not know her fate, nor her travail."
Then Pepin heard the pilgrim's woeful tale
And recognized the squire Blandyman!
Imploring him, he cried, "Now, if you can,
Pray tell me when her babes were born and lost."
"Why, Sire, it was the day our two paths crossed
Inside the wood. I told you of her plight.
In pride you put the blame on her outright!"
Astonishment made bright King Pepin's eyes
As, slowly, he began to realize
The foundling Valentine's identity,
That Orson, too, was born beneath the tree!
Remorse and joy were joined and Pepin wept
When he announced to all that he had kept
In his own house, as poor and penniless,
The sons of Alexander and the Empress
Bellisant! His proper nephews! Blandyman
Was shaken, more amazed than anyone
To learn, moreover, these had been the twain
Whom he had met outside of Aquitaine!
⌘ Now, in that land, Valentine could find no rest,
For visions of fair Clerymond and of his quest.
He took his leave from Savary, and sailed
With Orson on the sea until they hailed
A shining castle on an isle near Portugal.
They entered, after jousting with the seneschal.
When Clerymond first set her green-eyed gaze
On Valentine, I could recount the ways
She loved him, but to sum it up, I say
That Valentine was also smitten straightaway!
⌘ When she was told their mission, Clerymond
Led Valentine and Orson by the hand,

To seek the room that held the Oracle.
They found the door well guarded, by a churl
Who held an iron club, and by a lion,
It was said, would never harm the scion
Of an Emperor! Orson tossed the churl aside
And, entering the room, was stupefied
To see a chamber rich with gems and gilt.
Atop a golden pillar there was built
A priceless cabinet to hold the Brazen Head.
Valentine stepped near to open it and said,
"Pray, speak the truth of my nativity."
The Oracle replied with clarity:

"*Valentine, thou art the son of Alexander,*
*Emperor of Greece. Thy noble mother,*
*Bellisant, is sister to King Pepin.*
*Her husband cruelly banished her and in*
*The wood of Orléans, she soon gave birth*
*To thee, and to one other on this earth.*
*The fellow, Orson, that thou leadest here*
*Is thy twin brother. He was taken by a bear*
*That raised and nourished him. Unknowingly,*
*Thy uncle Pepin rescued thee that day*
*And nobly brought thee up. In much distress*
*Thy mother roamed. The giant Ferragus*
*Protected her for twenty years. Now, thou shall wed*
*The Lady Clerymond. And if thou cut the thread,*
*The bit of flesh that binds thy brother's tongue,*
*Then he shall speak as plain as anyone.*"

The Brass Head stopped and, verily, no sound
Was heard from it again. To Clerymond
The brothers' joy was evident: in gleeful cries
From Valentine and Orson's hearty sighs.
Transported by the truth, the two embraced;
All doubt of their identity had been erased. ❧

8

Friends, in the story
That you see today,
I, Pacolet, shall
Have a part to play.
I play myself!
For I was sent to schools
In Spain, and in Toledo
Learned the tools

And art of magic. By enchantment I have made
This flying horse of wood, and on its head
A pin is set, so I may guide its flight
Up or down, to and fro, or left and right.
As swift as any bird we ply the air!
Now, at the time it happened, I was there
When Clerymond was trothed to Valentine,
And I considered that it would be fine
To fly to Portugal on my enchanted horse
And tell these tidings to her brother, Ferragus.
This giant measured thirteen feet in height
And glowered down at me, an awesome sight,
With hair as stiff as bristles on a boar.
He listened, and his heart was wounded sore
To learn that Clerymond had made such vows
With Valentine, a knight whose ways and laws

Were foreign, who had vanquished, furthermore,
The Green Knight, their own brother. And he swore
To seek revenge. Of this he made no mention,
Better to accomplish his intention!
Instead, he smiled and said, "Tell Clerymond
That I am glad and soon I shall attend
Her wedding." I returned upon my route
And of his word or will I had no doubt
Until I had related all he said
To the good lady. She replied, with dread,
"Ah, Pacolet! I fear that Ferragus
Is angry and intends some harm to us.
I am afraid, because last night I dreamed
Of drowning in the sea, but then it seemed
A face appeared and saved me. Then I saw
A griffin issue from a cloud, and in its claw
It carried me away!" Valentine was there,
And led her to a flowered arbor, where
I heard him say, "My love, you must forget
Your fearful dream, for anyone who yet
Believes in dreams shall suffer all too much!"
Then Orson came to them, and with a gentle touch
They took away the thread of flesh that bound
His tongue. He was surprised to hear the sound

Of his own voice and spoke, with great delight,
Of his adventures, far into the night.
⌘ Now on the morrow Ferragus arrived,
And you shall see the plot that he contrived.
Valentine inquired, "Sir, I understand
That you have given refuge in your land
To one whose name is Bellisant. I yearn
With all my heart to see her, and to learn
If she may be my mother." "Possibly,"
The wily giant mused. "Come sail with me,
And in my castle you may interview
The lady, who will say if this is true.
If so, then you and Clerymond shall wed
In greater triumph there!" These words misled
The eager Valentine, who thought them kind,
For only love and faith were in his mind
As he and Orson sailed with Clerymond
Aboard her brother's ship. They were beyond
The sight of land, and in their berths at rest,
When Valentine and Orson, on behest
Of Ferragus, were bound and blindfolded,
Like men condemned to death. And it was said
That Clerymond protested bitterly!
She might have thrown herself into the sea

But was restrained, and not allowed one word
With either prisoner. The ship had moored,
And they were brought into the castle where
The Lady Bellisant, quite unaware
They were her children, heard they had been born
Near Paris, France. But more she could not learn,
Because the giant quickly had them cast
Into a dungeon, leaving them to fast
On bread and water. Clerymond confronted
Ferragus, who scolded her and ranted,
"You must forget these Frenchmen! They will die
As strangers to our ways!" Her bold reply
Was filled with mockery. "I shall, of course,
Obey. When I am thus constrained by force
All right is worthless, and necessity
The master of all virtue." But secretly
She counseled with her brother's kindly wife
And greeted Bellisant, about whose life
She knew the truth that very few had known.
The wondrous tidings of these words alone:
"Your children are alive and they are near!"
Were all that Bellisant had longed to hear.
But when she learned they were in prison there,
Her newfound joy, again, became despair.

⌘ Ah, friends, your Pacolet was much dismayed
To learn that Clerymond had been betrayed,
And hear that she blamed me! I said, "Dear Lady,
Trust that soon I shall devise some remedy.
I could not see into your brother's heart,
But shall avenge and serve you with my art,
And work enchantment with such subtlety
That you shall be content and pleased with me."
⌘ The night drew near and there were celebrations.
Ferragus, with all his lords and barons,
Made great cheer. But, when they wearied,
Went to bed, and slept, I quickly readied
All the gear to ply my craft. "Fie!" I said,
"On Ferragus!" and cast a spell that made
The prison gates fall open. In the darkness
Both the captives thought that I was Ferragus,
And Valentine knelt down to pray. But Orson
Called out, "I shall venge myself on anyone
Who lays a hand on us!" "Be not afraid!"
I shouted. "Come! For soon the night will fade
And day appear. Your mother waits!" We passed
The gates, and I threw charms on locks, and cast
My spells to keep the court asleep, until
Their mother had her two fair sons to fill
Her arms once more! The lady could not speak.
I thought such joy might cause her heart to break.
And when, indeed, she crumpled in a swoon,
The children held her tenderly. But soon
She rose, her arms around them, and she cried,
"My dearest ones. It cannot be denied
That we have suffered much. But by God's grace
You are alive, and here, in my embrace."
Then Valentine and Orson told their mother
All their deeds and perils, to that hour.
This was a joyful scene, but I had dread
Of vengeance from the giant, so I said,
"Dear Lady, leave this place and follow me!
I have a ship that waits you on the sea."
⌘ They sailed without delay for Aquitaine.
The giant woke, to hear his men complain
That by some mischief in the night, his own
Good sister, and the prisoners, had flown,
With Blandyman and Bellisant! He tore
His clothes, and in a crying rage, he swore
To take revenge, and followed after us.
Not yet had I outwitted Ferragus!

In furious pursuit,
The giant traced
Our route to Aquitaine
And there he placed
The city under
Siege. Duke Savary
And all his men fought
Well. Their bravery,
Assisted by the craft and cleverness,
If I may say, of Pacolet, forced Ferragus
To raise his siege and flee in disarray.
"Long life to Aquitaine!" they cheered. "Hooray!"
⌘ Once more the trumpets and the clarions
Resounded, now, so joyfully, for Orson's
Marriage to the Lady Fezon. Savary,
When told of Orson's noble ancestry,
Was more than glad, but sorry to report
That Pepin, with the Emperor, must have support,
Or both would die, besieged by enemies.
On hearing this, no solace could appease
The loyal Valentine, who vowed to bring relief.
His taking leave revived his mother's grief,
But he embraced her, promising to speak
So well on her behalf the Emperor would seek

His wife's forgiveness. Orson sweetly
Said to him, "I pray that God shall keep thee
Well and safe while we must be apart."
Each left his brother sorrowful in heart.
⌘ Friends, Valentine believed that only fools
Would trust in magic, that my skill and tools
Must be the Devil's work! But I gave promises
That my enchanted horse could carry us
To Constantinople in a single day!
"Mount up," I said. "Hold tight." We flew away
And swept above great cities, woods, and seas,
To seek the palace on the Golden Horn of Greece.
We entered the imperial hall when supper
Had been served to Pepin and the Emperor.
We both were much abashed at the degree
Of splendor in that court and company.
King Pepin shouted when he recognized
His nephew Valentine, and he apprised
The Emperor, "Your lineage lives on.
The knight you see before you is your son!"
These tidings caused the Emperor to pale
With thoughts of Bellisant. He stood to hail
Their son, beholding him with joy and pride.
A wave of cheers broke out on every side,

As Valentine was welcomed in the hall.
He raised his hand and said, before them all,
"I thank you, but my greatest thanks shall be
To my good uncle, who has cared for me.
To him I owe my life, although some say
It is to both our parents we must pay
The most respect and give allegiance more.
As for my father, whom I stand before,
I name myself an orphan of the wood.
I might have been discovered starved or dead
Had not my uncle found me. My mother,
Cruelly banished by the Emperor,
Is innocent of blame, and I shall fight
The false Archbishop, whosoever might
Accuse her of a wrong in any way!"
His father struggled through his shame to say,
"Alas! Alas! Dear son, there is no need.
The vile Archbishop has confessed his deed,
And he is dead. For long I tried, but failed,
To find your mother. Pray be kind, my child.
Tell me what you know." His son said, "Father,
Yesternight, it was, I spoke with her!
She lives in Aquitaine and she is well."
The grateful monarch bade that every bell

Resound to tell his joy. The noise alarmed
His foes encamped outside the walls, who armed
For an assault. The little and the great,
In tens of thousands, issued through the gate
To counter the attack. On every side
A multitude were wounded, many died,
Before the fight abated. I flew back
To Aquitaine, with news of this attack,
And with a letter sent to Bellisant
From Valentine. It gave her an account
Of how the Emperor, contrite of heart,
Still loved her, and was grieved to be apart.
❧ Now Orson, aided by Duke Savary,
Assembled men of arms and sailed the sea
Toward Greece. He led his wife, and Bellisant,
Whose own misgivings grew as the magnificent
And fabled domes of Constantinople rose
On the horizon. They drew near, and chose
To pass the harbor, for they planned to moor,
And set their camp in secret, on the shore.
❧ Good folk, your Pacolet is proud to mention
Powers of enchantment and invention
Saved the Emperor! I devised a plan
Whereby the added strength of Orson's men

Surprised the enemies, who met defeat.
A grateful Emperor went forth to greet
The men from Aquitaine, bestowing praise
And thanking each most heartily. His gaze
Soon fell on Orson. Valentine stepped near
And whispered, "Sire, your other son is here."
The Emperor took Orson in his arms and cried,
"By you my joy is doubled, hope is multiplied!"
Ah, there was ample cause to celebrate!
⌘ We rode in triumph through the Golden Gate
And to a fair pavilion by the sea,
Where Bellisant came out to greet our company.
The Emperor alighted from his horse,
As tears of tender yearning and remorse
Were spilling from his eyes. Without a word
These two embraced, who had been sundered
For a space of twenty years. The Emperor
Knelt down before his wife and said to her,
"Alas, my love, your suffering must weigh
Forever on my heart. I humbly pray
That you may pardon me for my great fault."
Then Bellisant spoke gently, deep in thought:
"My Lord, if I reprove you, I may lose
Occasion for our love, and so I choose

To dwell in joy and not in bitterness.
We have the gift of hours to redress
The hours lost. With thanks to Pacolet
And others, too, our sons are living yet!"
She lightened Pepin's heart with an embrace,
Rewarded the good merchant with a place
As chamberlain, and put her arms around
Her faithful squire, Blandyman! Profound
Emotions simple rhymes cannot express.
Our players show you bliss, and tenderness,
As family and friends are gathered home
Beneath the light of St. Sophia's dome. ❧

*This play has ended as the dark of night*
*Is drawing nigh. We players seek to light*
*These times on our good earth, when gifts*
*Of understanding heal the rifts*
*Of difference and fault. Bear witness,*
*Friends, to forces of forgiveness,*
*True devotion, and humility,*
*For they unite us as a family.*

# ABOUT VALENTINE & ORSON

. . . I am now encouraged to put this Old Story into a New Livery, and not to suffer that to lie Buried that a little Cost may keep Alive.

*From the publisher of the 1688 edition, London*

AMONG MY STUDIES as an art student at the University of Wisconsin–Madison was a course on the history of Flemish art, and one of the great masters whose work I came to cherish was Pieter Bruegel the Elder.

In May 1981, on my way to visit my daughter, Claire, near Salzburg, I stopped in Vienna to see the room in the Kunsthistorisches Museum in which many of Bruegel's most renowned paintings are gathered. Then, in February 1982, at the Boston Museum of Fine Arts, I viewed an exhibition of prints executed by the printer-publisher Hieronymous Cock to designs and drawings by Bruegel. Included in the exhibition was a woodcut titled *The Masquerade of Valentine and Orson*, sometimes titled *The Play of the Wild Man Hunt*. The subject of this print intrigued me enormously, and I was curious about its provenance and meaning. At the Boston Public Library, I found two important books, *Valentine and Orson: A Study in Late Medieval Romance* by Arthur Dickson, and *Valentine and Orson*, translated from the French by Henry Watson, edited by Arthur Dickson.

Over six centuries have passed since the hypothesized first version, a lost romance in French verse, given the name *Valentin et Sansnom*, was written by an unknown hand. All subsequent versions, in French, English, German, Dutch, Icelandic, Italian, and Spanish, are indebted to this source. A French prose version titled *Valentin et Orson* was printed at Lyons (c. 1475–89) by Jacques Maillet, and

one of the three surviving copies is in the Pierpont Morgan Library. Maillet's edition was translated into English by Henry Watson for Wynken de Worde (c. 1503–5), but this first English edition survives only as a black-letter fragment of four leaves. The one known, nearly complete, copy of the second edition (c. 1548–58) is in the Huntington Library. Seventy-five versions and variations in English have followed, the most recent in 1919. All are derived from Watson's translation.

The first half of Watson's *Valentine and Orson* closely parallels the Middle Low German verse version called *Valentin und Namelos* (c. 1400–50). This, in turn, is considered to be the closest to the lost French verse (c. 1300–50). Dickson explores the story's diverse sources and believes that it was based originally on a fairy tale.

*Valentine and Orson* is "an English prose romance of the Charlemagne cycle," and contains many of the literary conventions we expect in a tale of chivalry. However, reading it for the first time I was deeply affected by emotions and concerns that are as compelling today as they were then. Throughout the story I felt a sense of continuity and comradeship, and recognized a compassionate author akin to the caring and observant Bruegel.

Arthur Dickson assures us that, with few exceptions, Henry Watson's translation of

The Hystory of the
two valyaunte brethren Valentyne
and Orson, sonnes vnto the
Emperour of Grece

is "on the whole close but vigorous and idiomatic," while Watson himself pleads:

The whiche historye I Henrye Watson symple of vnderstondynge haue translated out of Frenche in to our maternall tongue of Englyshe, at the Instaunce of my worshypfull mayster Wynkyn de Worde. Prayeng all the reders or hearers here of to haue my youth for excused, yf I haue fayled in any thyng.

Henry Watson's translation has been my constant reference. After several drafts in prose, it was Chaucer's *Canterbury Tales* that prompted me to try the story in iambic pentameter couplets. It has been a lengthy and daunting process. Two hundred pages of Middle English prose have been winnowed in this interpretation to emphasize what is for me the essence of the story. I incorporated many expressions and phrases verbatim and echoed the text, but felt free to introduce variations. In words and paint, I have tried to remain faithful to, as well as to amplify, the spirit of *Valentine and Orson*.

The figure of the Wild Man belongs to the oldest elements of the story. Through the centuries he has been depicted in manuscript illuminations, sculpture, stained glass, metalwork, tapestries, coats of arms, playing cards, and choir stalls. In the seventeenth century, "Orson" was synonymous with "Wild Man." In 1804, the famous pantomimist Grimaldi made his first appearance at Covent Garden, playing Orson, in Thomas Dibdin's *Valentine and Orson: A Romantic Melo-drame*, which also toured in the United States. The Wild Man remains in the lore of many lands, East and West, and is a popular figure in modern-day festivals throughout Europe.

Valentine and Orson were the heroes of at least one lost Elizabethan play, dramas by Jakob Ayrer and Lope de Vega, and later became the subject of melodrama, burlesque, and pantomime.

It is because of Bruegel's print that I have always envisioned this tale as a play. The Wild Man appears again in Bruegel's painting *The Contest Between Carnival and Lent*, which, like *Children's Games* and *The Flemish Proverbs*, has a very high perspective, so that the picture plane is like a vast raked stage. Bruegel lived for several years in Antwerp, a center of artistic and festive life. He must have been influenced by dramatic performances in popular theater, as well as by the allegorical floats in Holy Day processions. He was a follower of the great humanist Erasmus, and would have agreed with Folly, in *The Praise of Folly*, observing from heaven what mortal men were up to: "There is no show like it. Good God, what a theater!"

I have imagined an itinerant band of players consisting of a family and their friend, the timeless Pacolet himself, traveling together in the countryside to play small villages, perhaps one of those that Bruegel depicted. Unlike the high scaffolds reached by ladders that we see in his prints and drawings, a low stage is set up so that one of the carthorses can be in the performance. Volunteers are recruited from among the villagers to complete the cast. This is far from a professional troupe, of which there were many in the Middle Ages. The costumes are makeshift, or worn castoffs from other companies. Props are invented with whatever comes to hand, although many, like the fireplace, backdrops, and other paraphernalia, are hauled in the cart. Weapons are represented by garden tools and kitchen utensils, Valentine's helmet being a lantern based on one in Bruegel's *Everyman*. This is a play presented by peace-loving people, and the artist himself comes to watch among the villagers.

It was not until the 1489 *Valentin et Orson* that Pacolet was introduced into the story. We are told that he was reared in Clerymond's castle in Portugal and that he learned his craft in Spain. I have imagined him as an Arab Muslim. I have given him another dimension as well; he is both enchanter and enchanted, weaving into and out of the centuries, as enchanters will.

While we cannot know what Pacolet signified for the unknown male or female author, I see him as a symbol of universality, a reminder of what European romance literature owes to contact with the East, the poetry and romances of the Arabs, their works on astrology, alchemy, magic, and divination. Pacolet is a bridge between East and West. He is welcomed to this play in his expanded role as narrator, poet, musician, and an actor who plays himself. We share King Pepin's awe when he watches Pacolet mount up into a great marble window, leap on his horse, turn the pin, and rise in the air like a tempest.

It is my hope that the verse, in the form of Pacolet's narration, which he speaks from offstage, will lend itself to reading aloud, an episode a night perhaps, the voice of the reader becoming an expressive, dramatic narrator, becoming Pacolet.

May there be readers, observers, and listeners of all ages who will enjoy, and carry forward, the story of *Valentine & Orson*.

I LAUD, WITH GRATITUDE, Floyd Yearout for vision, faith, and patience; Stephen Roxburgh for kind and thoughtful expertise; Robert Burkert for Sustenance; Family and Friends for aiding, abetting and forbearance; Susan Marsh for Grand Design; the late Stephen Harvard for his gift of warm encouragement; Fritz Eichenberg, whose engraving tool is mightier than the sword; Katy Homans; Professors John Wilde and James Watrous; all those who assisted at Farrar, Straus and Giroux; Rudolph Ellen-Bogan at the Butler Library, Columbia University; the helpful staff at the Pierpont Morgan Library; the University of Wisconsin-Milwaukee Golda Meir Library; and F. Schuyler Mathews for the song of the Hermit Thrush from *Field Book of Wild Birds and Their Music*.

*Nancy Ekholm Burkert*

BIBLIOGRAPHY

CLAESSONS, Rob, and Jeanne Rousseau. *Bruegel*. 1969. Reprint. New York: Alpine Fine Arts, 1981.

DICKSON, Arthur. *Valentine and Orson: A Study in Late Medieval Romance*. New York: Columbia University Press, 1929.

GIBSON, Walter S. *Bruegel*. New York: Oxford University Press, 1977.

HUSBAND, Timothy. *The Wild Man: Medieval Myth and Symbolism*. New York: The Metropolitan Museum of Art, 1980.

THORNDIKE, Lynn. *A History of Medieval Europe*. Boston: Houghton Mifflin, 1917.

WATSON, Henry, trans. *Valentine and Orson*. Edited by Arthur Dickson. 1937. Reprint. New York: Oxford University Press, 1971.

WYNDHAM, George. *The Springs of Romance in the Literature of Europe*. 1910. Reprint. Folcroft, Penn.: Folcroft Library Editions, 1973.

DESIGNED BY SUSAN MARSH & NANCY EKHOLM BURKERT

COMPOSED IN MONOTYPE DANTE BY MICHAEL & WINIFRED BIXLER

*Dante, a typeface of classic beauty and elegance, was designed by Giovanni Mardersteig in the mid-twentieth century.*
*Both the roman and the italic reflect Mardersteig's admiration for the letter forms of the Bolognese punchcutter Francesco Griffo,*
*who cut types for the scholar-printer Aldus Manutius in Venice at the turn of the sixteenth century.*

PRINTED IN ITALY BY MAZZUCCHELLI · MILAN

BOUND BY OLIVOTTO · VICENZA

COLOR SEPARATIONS BY SELE & COLOR · BERGAMO

PRODUCTION COORDINATED BY TRILOGY · MILAN

LIBRARY OF CONGRESS CATALOG CARD NUMBER: 89–45502

PUBLISHED SIMULTANEOUSLY IN CANADA BY COLLINS PUBLISHERS · TORONTO

FIRST EDITION · 1989